RUNAWAY TOMAT

To Adam and Jackson, for their bedtime story request,
and to Mike, for thinking big —K.C.R.

For Ronin and Theo —L.A.

DIAL BOOKS FOR YOUNG READERS
Published by the Penguin Group
Penguin Group (USA) LLC
375 Hudson Street
New York, New York 10014

USA / Canada / UK / Ireland / Australia / New Zealand / India / South Africa / China
penguin.com
A Penguin Random House Company

Reeder, Kim Cooley.
 Runaway tomato / by Kim Cooley Reeder ; pictures by Lincoln Agnew.
  p. cm.
 Summary: After dodging an enormous, rolling tomato, townsfolk hold a festival to honor the red fruit.
 ISBN 978-0-8037-3694-8 (hardcover)
 Special Markets ISBN 978-0-5254-3003-2 NOT FOR RESALE
 [1. Stories in rhyme. 2. Tomatoes—Fiction.] I. Agnew, Lincoln, ill. II. Title.
 PZ8.3.R253Ru 2014
 [E]—dc23   2012017935

Manufactured in China on acid-free paper
10 9 8 7 6 5 4 3 2 1

Designed by Lily Malcom
Text set in Grilled Cheese BTN

PEN / INK / DIGITAL / CROSS FINGERS

RUNAWAY TOMATO

by Kim Cooley Reeder

pictures by Lincoln Agnew

Dial Books for Young Readers

an imprint of Penguin Group (USA) LLC

Perfect day.
Full of light.

Rain, rain, rain
through the night.

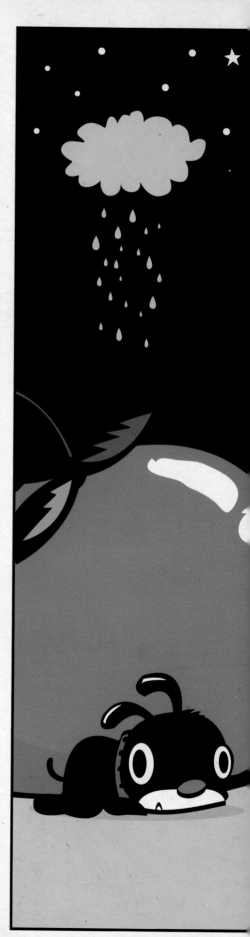

Tomato grows
big, big, big.
Door is stuck.
Get a rig.

Mower pulls.
Vroom, vroom, vroom.
Try the tractor.
Make some room.

Children coming.
Make the hike.
Bringing scooters,
wagons, bikes.

Hook them up
one by one.
Parents follow
on the run.

Tug and pull.
Push and shove.
Tomato's stuck.
Still won't budge.

Tow truck pulls
with all its might.
Whole town's here.
And what a sight!

Everyone push!
One, two, three!
Tomato slides.
Finally free.

Heads up! Move!
Look out below!
Tomato's rolling.
Won't go slow.

Faster, faster,
down it slides.
Hold on tight.
Oh, what a ride!

Police car comes.
Officers try.
Tomato zooms
right on by.

Firefighters!
On the double.
Ladder's raised.
Looks like trouble.

Firefighters
slip and slide
right on down
the tomato's side.

Far too slippery.
Can't hold tight.
Look, look, look!
A chopper's flight.

Chopper lowers
rope with hook.
Flies straight up.
Oh, no! Look!

Up, up, up
into the sky.
Tomato's going
high, high, high.

Rope is squeezing
much too tight.
Tomato's squishing.
What a sight!

Sauce is falling
down, down, down.
Like rain, rain, rain
across the town.

Yuck, yuck, yuck!
yells out the crowd.
It's like a bursting
tomato cloud.

Clean-up time
begins right here.
Everyone, now,
go get your gear.

Fill the wagons
to the brim.
Pickups waiting.
Dump it in.

Tractors plow up
fields of goo.
Mixer trucks,
collect your crew.

'Dozers push.
Backhoes dig.
Sauce fills up
ten red big rigs.

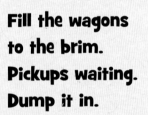

Garbage trucks,
your turn is here.
Back them up.
Put them in gear.

Fill the hopper
to the top.
Hopper's full.
Time to drop.

To the dump they
zoom, zoom, zoom.
Dump it out.
No more room.

Drive back down.
The work is done.
Mess cleaned up.
Now time for fun!

Darkness settles
on the square.
Tired people
everywhere,

strolling home
without a peep.
Work is done.
Town's fast asleep.

Rain, rain, rain
through the night.

Sun is shining
bright, bright, bright.

Tomatoes growing
at the dump.
No more room.

Bump.

bump.

bump.

Bumping, squishing
down the hill.
Grab the gear.
You know the drill.